"With God, All Things are Possible!"

Skookum Books Charms

The beautiful butterfly, that graces our flowers and bushes, goes through a mysterious and magical change in becoming an adult. The Greeks believed each time a butterfly emerges from its cocoon, a new human soul is born! Legend has it that whispering a wish to a butterfly, then releasing it to carry the wish to heaven, will make the wish come true! Perhaps this is when they acquire little clouds on their wings. The butterfly is a symbol of fresh life, happiness, and joy! The "night" butterfly, the moth, is attracted to a flame and light, just like our souls are attracted to heavenly truths!

Hummingbirds are active, beautiful additions to our gardens, who give us a sense of life, nature's beauty, and fresh life! These "flying jewels" flit from flower to flower, picking up and delivering pollen, so that life can continue. Hummingbirds open the heart and show the truth of beauty! It brings laughter and enjoyment and the magic of being alive! The hummingbird stands for spreading love and joy!

Dedication: To our middle son, Stephen, who provided many wonderful experiences, using his many talents. He cared for those around him and devoted his young life to helping others. He never took a job, based on money. His summers were devoted to helping the youth. He was a wonderful and positive influence as a brother. Everything he did as a young man was a success, from playing baseball, football, and track to playing Curly in Oklahoma, and Tommy in Brigadoon. He had a beautiful voice and left unforgettable memories and lasting impressions! He was ever thoughtful of others!

Acknowledgements: My teaching, after my family, was the love of my life. I count it as a blessing to me to have had the privilege to teach the wonderful children at Madison Elementary School, in Sandusky, Ohio.

A Medley of Options for the "Not Yet Old" Set

Table of Contents

A Medley of Options For the "Not Yet Old" Set

Betty Lou Rogers

Growing

Have you ever thought about your life,
The many choices you have to make?
You were growing each day, as babies do,
But you had to cry, when you needed aid!

And as you grew, you socialized,
You thought with innocence so pure,
You accepted the love that was offered you,
The love from your parents, made you feel so secure!

As you're growing, you began to learn,
Of the kind of choices to make,
You discovered all things were not the same,
You found some were real, others were fake!

If you did slip up, and do something wrong,
At the time, it sounded exciting and fun,
But someone was hurt because of such tricks,
Made you think your actions were stupid and dumb!

Have you ever wondered about your life,
Is there a reason why you are here?
Who might be helped because you lived,
What good deed was done, because you were near?

Growing up is not always easy to do,
It's fraught with anger, tears, and torment,
There's lots of wonderment, joy, and fun,
For this journey you're on, with good intent!

Decide real soon the direction you'll go,
Choices of good, bad, easy, or hard,
Your life will be what you make of it,
Make the right choices, and stay in charge!

Sometimes "easy" sounds real good,
Many times "hard" does not,
If you always look for the easiest way,
You could end up being the "id - i - ot!

If you believe your life could be better,
You should find what things you can change,
Seek advice, study hard, learn all you can,
A happier life, can come from a life rearranged!

Ben Franklin was a wise. old man,
The advice he gave was the best,
"Making an investment in knowledge,
Always pays the best interest!"

God gave us a beautiful, glorious world,
Filled with goodness and wonders so rare,
Where love and kindness and truth abide,
Fills you with happiness and peace inside!

Happiness is as close as your elbow,
Extend it, and lend a helping hand,
Lift it up, and send friendly greetings,
Shows love, when a shoulder it's squeezing!

Feelings

Feelings are so very important,
They help us feel our worth,
Good feelings nourish and strengthen our hearts,
It lifts to new heights, for the love it imparts!

Do you feel happy, like everyone should?
You were meant to be joyful in life,
Look for those things that are righteous and true,
And joy and happiness will even find you!

Why wouldn't everyone want to be happy?
Happy is fun, it really feels grand,
Happy is pleasant, it fills with delight,
And when you share happy, it's even more right!

If you're not happy, find out why,
Are you feeling empty, alone, or afraid?
Are you making wrong choices, following bad advice?
Explore what is good, let that be your guide!

Winning

Winning is wonderful, it's lots of fun,
It makes us feel, oh, so accomplished,
With hard work, winning's beyond compare,
But only, if you've won it, playing fair and square!

If you claim a win, but you had to cheat,
And someone else lost, playing fair,
Then it's not a win, you must realize,
Are you going to take home that person's prize?

Could you ever enjoy taking a prize,
That hadn't been earned, playing fair?
Why would you want to have it around?
Wouldn't it remind you, the win wasn't sound?

You work real hard, you want to win,
But you never come out on top,
We all were born with different skills,
We all must find our spot to fill!

Winners respect their fellowman,
They are gracious and thankful for life,
Winners don't boast, or brag, or tease,
They're truthful and honest and aim to please!

If you work real hard to win,
And you're just, and fair, and true,
You "are" the best, you follow rules,
You are a winner, through and through!

Losing!

Now losing a contest, and accepting with grace,
Is a righteous and wholesome endeavor,
To admire and respect the talents of others,
Is a winner, showing outstanding behavior!

Losing is the pits, it's a disaster in the making,
It can send you into a dark, scary loop,
It makes you feel that you're no good,
You think you're the worst one in your group!

But you absolutely are not the worst,
You could be the best somewhere else,
You must find, for yourself, where is that place?
Seek advice, use your brain, hard work embrace!

Never give in to weakness or sin,
Be strong, search real hard for your strength,
You do have worth, it's in your heart,
Engage, work hard, be unyielding and smart!

But if you grow weary and full of doubt,
You want to be someone worth noting,
So what do you do when you feel so defeated?
"Treat others the way you'd like to be treated!"

It's Magic!

Did you know you can perform magic?
You can actually make things disappear!
If you've hurt a friend with unkind words,
Wave your wand, apologize, and be sincere!

If you've been thoughtless and careless,
And harmed someone, caused them distress,
Those words and actions will disappear,
If you zap your love, and be sincere!

If someone has made you unhappy,
By allowing their temper free reign,
You can rid out, do away with, even banish,
Your forgiveness will make everything vanish!

If you have hurt someone's feelings,
And you really wished you had not,
Just open up your own magic potion,
And rub it on with nurturing devotion!

Don't be a cheater, it's the lowest to go,
You might think it's the only way to play,
But cheating is lying, it's stealing as well,
With this kind of behavior, you'll never excel!

If you think cheating is the way to compete,
You must know, in everyway, that it's wrong,
You've stolen from someone to reward yourself,
Your feelings of achievement can't be very strong!

When you cheat, you really haven't won,
You've taken the prize from another,
So you cannot feel, that you are the best,
When you lied before God, and all the rest!

When someone cheats, and then gets caught,
They're ready to blame someone else,
Who in the world would "make" them cheat?
When did they lose control of themselves?

Finally, you decide what you did was wrong,
Will you admit it, or make an excuse?
It's best to say, "I made a mistake",
Admit you were wrong, and clean the slate!

If you do something wrong, it's but one wrong,
If you lie about it, that makes two,
If you try to hide it, and blame someone else,
That makes four wrongs, all due to you!

For a person to be a true winner,
They should be thoughtful, humble, and kind,
But, a loser can also be a victor,
By showing respect and an unselfish mind!

Hating!

The sad, bad feeling in our world today,
Is the hate that consumes all the fools,
Hate destructs, it destroys, and defiles,
It's reckless, evil, and oh, so vile!

Hating absolutely does no good,
And it destroys the person who hates.
The hater is filled with demons so dark,
Hate hurts, and haunts, leaves a terrible mark!

Now, haters have deep ugly scars,
That you won't find in a world full of love,
It certainly doesn't make a bit of sense,
To not want fun, and prefer violence!

Are you a person who argues a lot?
Do you, with others, often disagree?
Is it hard for you to handle problems?
You might need guidance immediately!

Honor!

Honor is the value you place in yourself,
You forgive others, you're honest, and just,
You shun all evil, you're fair to a fault,
You are dependable, keep promises, and trust!

Set your goals high for what to achieve,
Be responsible, dependable, and true,
Will you aid, assist, promote goodwill?
Can you remain humble, and still be you?

Honorable is when you refuse to accept,
Those who are cheating and don't tell the truth,
It is better to leave them, they only cause strife,
You're above all that, you choose goodness in life!

Have you ever wondered why you're here?
Perhaps to comfort, care, and console?
To watch over those so troubled by grief,
To nurture the homeless, and give them relief!

Goodness!

If you find you want goodness to reign,
And you feel heartfelt faith in your Maker,
He gave us the freedom to choose for ourselves
But, He wants us to be givers, not takers!

Being strong is cherishing your values,
You're saying there's things you won't do,
You have to be brave and stick to your plan,
Being a good person, brings a life that is grand!

Wisdom is knowing what doesn't belong,
There are actions and deeds that are wrong,
Evil helps no one and it wrecks the weak,
Be the strong person for the good, all should seek!

Being righteous is becoming involved,
In the lives of those needing your care,
Are you ready to help, to assist, and to share,
Are you willing to spread your love everywhere?

When you accept goodness, you'll find right away,
There is happiness, contentment, and fun,
There's laughing and joking, and unfettered joy,
And the freedom you'll feel has been won!

But if you are foolish, and accept what's not true,
Or even what's harmful and wrong,
Your life will be crowded with demons untold,
Misery and fears will follow, until you are old!

When you see something that's really wrong,
And others ignore it, and look aside,
Will you too, turn your back, and look away?
Or will you take a stand against evil each day?

Common Sense!

Whatever happened to good common sense?
When evil threats are made to our homes,
And ugly people want to end our lives,
Is it logical and reasonable to think they won't?

Where did sound and practical understanding go?
When evil people show hate and jealous pride,
Does it make sense to think they will change,
And become a part of our peaceful life?

We must be aware, there are people about,
Who want to change our way of life,
We must stand firm and obey our laws,
And keep our country free and strong

A person is only as good as their word,
If you say that you're honest, then be it,
If you make a promise, then keep it,
If you stand for truth, then show it!

Loving!

Love is like a sandwich,
It's the meat inside the bun,
It nourishes rather quickly,
And you can use it on the run!

Love rejoices with a nice warm smile,
Love protects when it cares and forgives,
Love endures when it calms all our fears,
Love performs when it wipes away all tears!

Love and affection are what we all need,
It makes us feel, oh so, secure,
Do everything you can to share and be kind,
And our world will improve, and be superfine!

What is it like to be without love?
Like a joyful song bird, who cannot sing,
Like a shiny, silver bell, that has lost its ring,
Like a beautiful butterfly, with a broken wing!

Contentment is yours for the taking,
You can find it in your own backyard,
The sweet sounds and beauty of nature,
Can touch you and gladden your heart!

Love's not selfish, proud, or rude,,
Love doesn't tally the times it's used,
It's not jealous, it's full of hope,
Love protects, and it will not boast!

Love's more important than anything else,
It's at the very top of God's list,
Love directs us, protects us, sets us free,
Free to live in peace and harmony!

Love is the greatest quality to have,
When dispensed, it covers like paint,
Love has much power because it can heal,
Love creates miracles, and miracles are real!

Love involves us in other's lives,
Love shows us where we are needed,
Love can lead and guide our every endeavor,
Love is the glue that binds us together!

Have you ever thought how lucky you are?
For a healthy body, and parents who care?
You've hit the jackpot, the pot of gold,
But, do you know it? Are you really aware?

Cowards!

You are a coward, if you can't stand the truth,
Or you won't change, when you're proven wrong
When you won't listen or take good advice,
When you won't stand for righteousness in your life!

Fools die a thousand deaths,
The treacherous will destroy themselves,
Opportunists will be trapped in their very own greed,
They're all wrapped in chains, not meeting their needs!

Are you a coward or a brave soul,
Do you lead from the front or the back?
Are you brave enough to admit what you lack?
Are you smart enough, to offer others some slack?,

Anytime someone is named the champ,
And they aren't the real winner at all,
How many cowards remain in their seats?
They aren't getting up, not standing too tall!

Right is right, and wrong is wrong,
No truer words were spoken,
If things are right for a certain group,
Then they should be right for everyone!

Right is right, and wrong is wrong,
There is no in-between
,It's either wrong for everyone
Or right, when all is said and done!,

Some people think they're above the law,
They think they are better than others,
Better in looks, talking, or wealth?
Probably, better in thieving and stealth!

Being Your Own Person!

When you see something needs to be done,
Do you get busy and do it yourself?
That's what a responsible person will do,
You're being reliant, dependable, honest, and true!

Do you know how to solve problems?
Do you know different "hows" and "ways"?
Do you follow rules to complete a task?
Can you find fair answers for those who ask?

When you have to make a decision,
Do you seek experts who are smart?
Do you consider customs that work for good?
Do you study it, as well you should?

The next thing to do, when trying to decide,
Look at which answers make sense,
Think of past experiences, and proven facts,
You'll come up with answers, which are exact!

Teachers have a serious task on their hands,
To guide, counsel, and direct all around,
Teachers who teach "what" to think, are wrong,
Students need to learn "how" to think, that's sound!

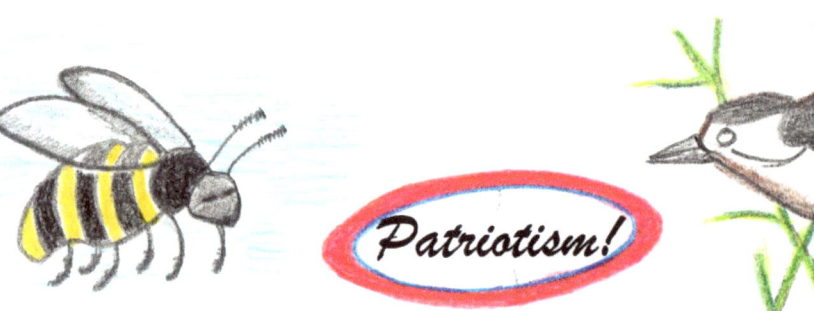

Patriotism!

Would you be the one to keep our country free?
Would you fight all those, who lie and disagree?
Will you stand for goodness, truth, and honesty?
Would you live for righteousness, and do it earnestly!

God gave us the right to be happy,
He gave us the right to feel free,
He didn't give anyone the right to decide,
To ruin our country with self-centered greed!

The politicians who rant and rave,
They make promises, not ever kept,
They end up being, all talk no action,
All this pontificating brings no satisfaction!

In life, there's always a better way,
A better way to work, a better way to play,
And better thoughts and better actions,
Will bring to mind, many better attractions!

Have you ever thought, when you're gone from this earth,
Of what people are liable to say?
Will they feel they've been lucky having known you?
Will it be for the many good deeds that you do?

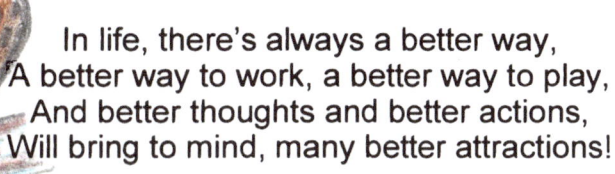

Humans Are Different!

Humans show much love and concern
,They need each other's help and care,
They feel responsible, they think with ease,
Animals think only of themselves, if you please!

People work so very hard,
To keep their families safe and well,
They learn, and play, and worry some,
Animals are concerned with food and fun!

People go to school to learn,
They make things, and can repair,
They grow in wisdom, truth, and grace,
They honor goodness, and know their place!

Animals don't kill because of spots and stripes,
Jealousy is not a reason to take a life,
Animals kill for food, not fun,
Yet, people kill their companions!

Thinking is common to humans,
Animals don't think this same way,
But, sometimes, humans do not think,
This is when humans tend to stray!

Your Maker and You!

God's spirit shows up in your feelings,
It encompasses all the love there can be,
All that's required is loyalty and faith,
And the courage to be wholesome and free!

The rainbow's the way God signs His name,
His signature is there, all can see,
He made us a promise, He kept His Word,
When you look at a rainbow, it's God's guarantee!

Everyone should be filled with happiness,
There are many ways to find joy in your life,
Nurturing, caring, and sharing with all,
Living and loving, God making the call!

And then, when you see that poor lost soul,
Who is hungry and scantily clad,
Who has no family, friends, warm pillow, or bed,
They need comfort, care, your love and respect!

Goals are finish lines you want to reach,
You'll make many turns along the way,
You'll find some hurdles, others a piece of cake,
You'll win with God's help, and the choices you make!

Lighten up, brighten up, look into the sky,
Ask your Maker what He wants,
Use your struggles to make you strong,
Find the wisdom to right some wrongs!

By wanting and choosing what's right in our world,
You're being so good to yourself,
You'll find there's power in wisdom and love,
You're arming yourself, with some strength from above!

The older you grow, the more choices there are,
You have to think wisely and well,
You must be alert, and awake, and aware,
Turn down the choices which are wrong and unfair!

What will last as time passes on?
Love is the content of God's message to us,
Hope is the attitude we hold so dear,
Faith is the charm that frees us from fear!

If ever you want to make others feel worthy,
And show them you really do care,
Just light up your face with a sunny smile,
And send friendly greetings, to all, everywhere!

And always remember - - - Never forget:

America is your homeland,
'Twas won with blood and strife,
And cherish all our freedoms,
And guard them with your life!

About the Author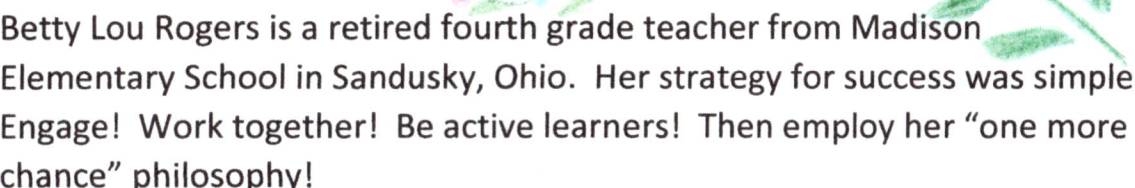

Betty Lou Rogers is a retired fourth grade teacher from Madison Elementary School in Sandusky, Ohio. Her strategy for success was simple. Engage! Work together! Be active learners! Then employ her "one more chance" philosophy!

Betty Lou Rogers grew up in rural northwestern Ohio, graduating from Fremont Ross High School. She married her childhood sweetheart and raised three sons. During this time, she returned to college where she graduated with a B. S. Degree in Elementary Education from Bowling Green State University, in Bowling Green, Ohio. She was a member of the prestigious educational society, Kappa Delta Pi.

While teaching at Madison School, Mrs. Rogers was keenly aware of what children needed, both as a group and as individuals, in effectual learning in the classroom. She also had the intuition to know how to accomplish this by challenging her students to be active learners, as opposed to the sit, listen, and absorb approach! Always have lesson material in front of the student, so they are actively participating in the lesson, never pushing the child beyond their ability, but always working toward the best they can do! Often times the student is awakened to and surprised by their own ability. Mrs. Rogers' most telling educational approach was offering the children "one more chance" to learn and succeed, by giving open-book tests!

Tests show what the student hasn't learned! "My job is to give the children every opportunity to learn." This strategy caused her students to become more familiar with the contents and location of information in their books. This offering, enabled them to find the answer, complete the test, and learn what was missed before. These answers could even be more meaningful to them! When parents found this out, there was no excuse for a failing grade!

Mrs. Rogers was also a Jennings Scholar, which honored and rewarded teachers in the elementary classroom. The Jennings Foundation provides a means for greater accomplishment, on the part of teachers, with the hope it would result in greater recognition for those in the teaching profession within the public school system.

Mrs. Rogers and her husband chose to retire in beautiful South Carolina. They are members of Advent United Methodist Church in Simpsonville, S.C. Besides writing, she loves her sewing and crafts, and gardening! Mrs. Rogers and her husband have four granddaughters, and seven great-grandchildren! After twenty-seven years of teaching, Mrs. Rogers philosophy for success has permeated the American landscape through her students in both academic and professional fields. Her love for teaching and writing, can never be equaled in any way, except her hope for students to find her writing truly illuminating!

New publications coming:

Kate Earns Her MBA in Manners, Behavior, Attitude!

Chris Earns His MBA in Manners, Behavior, Attitude!

Acquiring The Human Skills of Thinking, Saying, and Doing, for Teens!

A Medley of Options for the "Not Yet Old" Set!

God and Country. Two Sets of Laws For Teens!

The Human Dilemma of the Young, The Scramble for Power, Approval, and Money, (Ecclesiastes)

Teens, Consider the Circumstances and Consequences!

Law and Order for Teens: Ignore or Restore!

ABC's For Teens, and What They Mean!

Loves Flowers, Hates Weeds!

So, You Think We Shouldn't Have Dropped "The Bomb"?

For fun: Bossy Susie Saucy   and Capricious Caleb O'Connor

www.ingramcontent.com/pod-product-compliance
Lightning Source LLC
Chambersburg PA
CBHW041556120626
46551CB00002B/223